For Noah & Ivy,
Emily & Isabel, and Jude –
what a lovely bunch!

First U.S. edition 2015

Library of Congress Catalog Card Number 2014949715
ISBN 978-0-7636-7956-9

15 16 17 18 19 20 TLF 10 9 8 7 6 5 4 3 2 1
Printed in Dongguan, Guangdong, China

This book was typeset in Ellington MT and Seasoned Hostess.
The illustrations were done in ink and wash.
Edited by Libby Hamilton
Designed by Mike Jolley

TEMPLAR BOOKS

an imprint of
Candlewick Press
99 Dover Street
Somerville, Massachusetts 02144
www.candlewick.com

Troll and the Oliver

Adam Stower

templar books
an imprint of Candlewick Press

This is Troll.

And this is an Oliver.

Every day around lunchtime . . .

Troll tries to eat the Oliver.

But catching an Oliver is a tricky business.
No matter how hard Troll tried,
he could never quite manage it.

And the Oliver was never any help at all.

Instead of standing
nice and still,

the Oliver ran around
all over the place,

which made grabbing it
very difficult.

Each time Troll got close,

the Oliver would suddenly vanish.

And for something normally so LOUD and SQUEAKY,

it would choose just the wrong moment . . .

Even when Troll was sure he'd finally,
definitely, ABSOLUTELY caught the Oliver . . .

he hadn't.

By spring, Troll was grumpy,
tired, and very, very hungry.

It just wasn't fair. It was almost as if the Oliver
was doing it on purpose.

Troll went back to his hole
and ate his dinner of twigs and stones.

He'd had enough of pesky Olivers.

The next morning, Oliver fetched
his basket and set off to go shopping as usual.
He took extra care through the woods,
expecting Troll to jump out
at any moment.

But he didn't.

On the way back,
Oliver checked the long grass in the meadow
to see if Troll was hiding there,
waiting to grab his ankles.

He wasn't.

Then he tiptoed across the bridge,

just in case.

But there
was no sign
of Troll
anywhere.
It was most
peculiar.

In fact, Oliver didn't see Troll all day long,
and soon he was safely home again.

It wasn't until Oliver was busy in the kitchen
that he suddenly understood.

Troll had given up!
He was gone forever!

OLIVER HAD WON!

He felt exceedingly
pleased with
himself.

Troll felt exceedingly pleased with himself.

But unluckily for Troll

and luckily for
Olivers everywhere . . .

Olivers taste **REVOLTING!**

BLEEEUGHHHH!

Poor Troll.

He was hungrier than ever.

Troll slumped and sighed. Oliver sat and dripped.

tick, tick, tick,

But just then they heard a *tick, tick, tick,*

PING!

And from that moment on, everything changed.

These days Troll is never hungry,

and he doesn't have to eat stones or twigs . . .

or Olivers, thank goodness!

Author's Note

I would strongly advise the reader
to ALWAYS have some cake handy,
just in case a troll should happen by.
He might be hungry. . . .

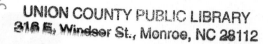

TROLLIVER'S COOKBOOK

Troll Cupcakes

(Makes 12 cupcakes)

Ingredients

For the Cupcakes

- ½ cup butter, softened
- ½ cup sugar
- 2 eggs
- 1 tsp. vanilla extract
- ½ cup flour

For the Frosting and Decorations

- ½ cup butter, softened
- 2½ cups confectioner's sugar
- A few drops of food coloring
- Shredded coconut
- Raisins, mini marshmallows, and/or assorted candies for decorating

Directions

For the Cupcakes

1. Ask a grown-up to preheat the oven to 350°F.
2. Line a 12-cup muffin tin with paper liners.
3. In a large bowl, cream the butter and sugar together to make a smooth, pale mixture.
4. Beat in the eggs a little at a time, then stir in the vanilla extract. (You might need some troll help for the beating—it means stirring really hard and fast.)
5. Using a big metal spoon, mix in the flour.
6. Spoon the mixture evenly into the muffin cups until they are half full.
7. Ask a grown-up to put the muffin tin in the oven and bake the cupcakes for 10-15 minutes, until they're golden brown on top.
8. Let them cool in the muffin tin for 10 minutes, then on a wire cooling rack.